D0450438

EJ12
GIRL HERO

First American Edition 2015
Kane Miller, A Division of EDC Publishing

Cover illustrations by Dyani Stagg

First published by Scholastic Australia Pty Limited in 2010
This edition published under license from Scholastic Australia Pty Limited on behalf of Lemonfizz Media

For information contact:
Kane Miller, A Division of EDC Publishing
P.O. Box 470663
Tulsa, OK 74147-0663
www.kanemiller.com
www.edcpub.com
www.usbornebooksandmore.com

Library of Congress Control Number: 2014949841

Printed and bound in the United States of America
2 3 4 5 6 7 8 9 10

ISBN: 978-1-61067-384-6

ROCKY ROAD

7-8-7-2-6-6-2-4
6-2-3-2-7-5-2-6-3

3-6-7 3-3-8-2-7-3

Chapter 1

Emma and Elle spun themselves around Emma's bedroom, singing and dancing to the latest Pink Shadows song. Emma was trying out a new dance move and Elle was singing passionately into a hairbrush. They had raided both Emma's closet and her dress-up box and the resulting look was a combination of crazy fairy and rock chick: black jeans, old tutus, heaps of bangles and necklaces and, as a finishing touch, sparkling tiaras. They had also been working on a dance routine and when the song reached the chorus, Emma and Elle were back to back, singing at the top of their voices.

We're gonna rock.
It's our time to shine.
Yeah our time is now!
Don't say don't,
Don't say wait.
We're gonna rock,
We're gonna shine!

The song finished and they both collapsed on the beanbag, laughing and exhausted. Emma's older brother, Bob, burst in.

"Are you two okay?" asked Bob, with a broad grin on his face. "Do you need medical help? Oh, I see, you were singing. Sorry, I thought you were in pain."

"Hilarious, Bob, see you!" and with that Emma shut the door, perhaps a little too loudly.

"Brothers!" said Emma. "Ugh!"

"Tell me about it," said Elle, who had two of

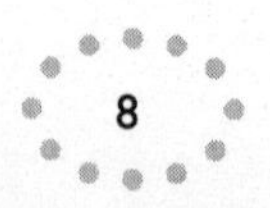

them. "But that was fun, Em, wasn't it? It was the best."

"Well, maybe not quite the best," said Emma. "If it was really the best, we would have been eating chocolate too."

"True," agreed Elle. "And we would be going to the Pink Shadows concert. They are playing here this week. How much fun would that be?"

"Tickets sold out months ago," sighed Emma, "and even if there were some left, I'm not sure Dad would let me go."

"Mine wouldn't either," replied Elle, "but at least we have our band practice tomorrow."

"Yes! I'd forgotten that," said Emma. "Maybe we can teach the others our dance routine. It will be great for the band. Come on, let's do it one more time."

So the girls got up and did it all over again, adding a few more moves and loving every minute of it. Elle kept thinking of new steps to add to the routine and teaching Emma, who was amazed how her friend just came up with all these crazy moves.

Emma loved music, she loved playing it, she loved listening to it and she loved dancing to it. She loved it when she was happy; she would sing at the top of her voice and bounce around the room. She liked it when she was sad; she would listen to slow songs over and over, thinking how terrible everything was, until, that is, she cheered up again. When she was angry she would strum her guitar strings so hard it hurt her fingers. Whatever her mood, Emma loved the way music could match it and how it expressed her feelings.

She loved playing music with other people too. She and her friends had formed a band. This week it was called Squishy Music, but last week it was called Beat Girls and the week before that it was, rather randomly, called We ♥ Penguins.

The girls' school had band instruments and students were allowed to sign up and use them in the music room. The girls had a regular Monday lunchtime practice. Emma was lead guitar and Hannah was bass guitar, Elle was keyboard and Isi, Isi was drums. It was the only instrument that could cope with her excitement levels. All the girls took turns to sing, although Emma was happy to let the others take the lead; she was content playing in the background.

After Elle had gone home, Emma sat on her bed playing her guitar. Her puppy, Pip, and her kitten, Inky, were on either side of her. She started playing the opening bars of the Pink Shadows song but then wandered into playing a tune she was making up herself. She hummed along as one hand moved along the neck of the guitar while she picked through the strings with her other. Pip and Inky were not the most attentive audience, indeed they were fast asleep and that was just fine with Emma.

Emma much preferred her music to be something she did by herself or, at least, something she shared with just a few friends. She didn't really like performing or being in the spotlight. She didn't mind the clapping and cheering that came at the end of the performance, although her mom sometimes got a bit carried away which was embarrassing, but she didn't really enjoy performing in front of people.

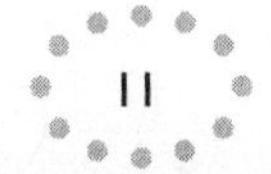

It was frightening. Emma would freeze, she couldn't play a note and she forgot all the words. While her friends, especially Elle, seemed to love performing in public, Emma preferred to keep her music a secret. She liked to keep it as something which was shared with only a few special people. Which wasn't such a surprise really. After all, she was a secret agent.

Emma Jacks was Special Agent EJ12, field agent and expert code-cracker in the under-twelve division for the SHINE agency. SHINE uncovered and stopped the plans of the evil agency *SHADOW*. To do that, SHINE needed agents, code-cracking agents, and EJ12 was one of their very best, despite still being in elementary school.

Emma had been recruited to SHINE when she won a math competition. SHINE used math competitions to help them find people who could think well and solve problems. When Emma was

introduced to SHINE, she thought they must have made a mistake–she did like math, but she didn't think she was very good at solving problems at all. In fact, she always seemed to be having problems rather than solving them. However, as EJ12, she had solved many problems, cracked lots of codes and stopped *SHADOW's* evil plans. She had saved rain forests, shut down *SHADOW* spy bases and rescued wild animals. SHINE hadn't made a mistake. In fact, as EJ12, Emma Jacks was one of their best agents and in the top five of the SHINE Shining Stars Spy of the Year competition.

SHADOW also had good agents and they had them all over the world. They communicated with them via secret messages. They left notes, they sent emails and texts, once they even carved a code into a tree in the middle of a rain forest. They were always coming up with new ways to give instructions to their agents so they could carry out their evil plans.

If SHINE was going to stop *SHADOW*, they had to intercept their messages, crack their codes and try

to keep one step ahead of them. Normally SHINE managed to keep *SHADOW* under control, but lately they had been having problems tracking down the messages. They suspected that *SHADOW* must have found a new way to send out their messages but couldn't discover what that was. It must have been music to *SHADOW's* ears.

SHADOW might have changed their tune, however, if they knew that EJ12 was about to take on the mission.

Emma had barely gotten to school the next morning when Hannah, Isi and Elle raced up to her. Isi, predictably, nearly knocked Emma down in her excitement.

"You'll never guess what has happened," cried Hannah.

"It is the best thing ever!" cried Elle.

"It is so cool, so, so cool!" shrieked Isi.

"What?" asked Emma. "What's happened?"

And then everyone started talking at once.

"It's a competition," said Elle.

"A music competition!" shrieked Isi, once again getting herself rather worked up.

"We've Got Talent," said Hannah.

"Well, we are *quite* good," began Emma, wondering why Hannah would suddenly declare how good she thought they were.

"No, We've Got Talent is the competition! You know, like on TV. The school is having its own talent competition and we *have* to enter our band. We get to perform in front of the whole school," explained Hannah.

"And our families are invited too," said Elle. "How good is that? It will be like we're a real band, at a real concert."

Emma looked at her friends. Hannah, Elle and Isi were beaming because they were all so excited at the thought of performing at the competition, but Emma was worried. She loved playing with her friends, but the idea of performing in front of lots of people scared her. What if she messed up the performance? What if she let her friends down? Emma still remembered the kindergarten concert where everyone was singing, "If you're happy and you know it, clap your hands." Everyone except Emma, who was not happy and was not clapping her hands. She had just stood there, mouth open, eyes wide with fright, staring out into the audience, not singing a word, and then bursting into tears, ruining the performance. She felt that she'd let everyone down then. Would she do it again at the talent competition? She would hate to let down her friends.

"It's a fantastic idea, don't you think, Em?" said Isi.

"Maybe we can wear the costumes we created at your house," said Elle. "We will rock!"

"Yeah, it's great," said Emma trying, rather unsuccessfully, to sound as thrilled as the others. But it was no good, she had to tell her friends. "Except what if I can't do it?" said Emma.

"Do what?" asked Elle.

"The competition," replied Emma.

"Why not, are you going to be away?" asked Hannah looking confused.

"No, I'll be here, but what if I can't perform, you

know, on stage in front of everyone. You guys are all so excited about it, but I'm nervous that I'll get stage fright and freeze and ruin it for us," said Emma, her eyes stinging a bit. *Oh no,* she thought, *I am not going to cry as well, am I? What a baby!*

Elle must have sensed her friend was getting a little upset because she put her arm around Emma.

"Why wouldn't you be able to do it, Em?" asked Elle. "We play all the time and you love it."

"And you're great," said Hannah.

"Yes, but then it's just us. This is in front of the whole school," said Emma.

"And all our families," piped in Isi.

"Isi, that's not helpful," said Hannah.

"But Isi is right, there *will* be lots of people. What if I just freeze and mess everything up?"

"But it's no different from a gymnastics meet, is it? You don't worry about people watching then," said Elle.

That was a good point, and typical of Elle to be so logical, but somehow it was just different. Emma couldn't explain why.

The school bell went and the girls bounced into their classrooms, still bubbling with excitement. Only Emma was a little less bouncy than the rest of them.

At lunchtime, everyone was still talking about the talent competition. The entire school was completely obsessed with it and almost everybody was going to be performing. On the playground, everyone was arranging groups and talking about what they might do. Some kids were going to dance, some sing a song and some were going to do magic tricks. One boy was going to burp the entire alphabet.

"That is so gross," announced Nema who had just flounced by. "Of course I don't know why anyone else is bothering, or at least bothering to try winning the competition. I think we already know who is going to win."

"Squishy Music!" cried Isi.

"Oh really," said Nema, "I don't think so, Dizzy."

Dizzy was one of Isi's nicknames; she got it because she was always running around so much that people thought she must get dizzy. Dizzy Isi. It was funny when her family and friends used it, but Nema made it sound mean. Isi glared at Nema, who glared back.

"Whatever," Nema said. "My band will just be too, too good, too pretty, too awesome. We should probably be entering the competition on television, not just this silly little school one."

"What's your band called, Nema?" asked Hannah.

"Oh, I thought you knew, I thought everyone knew—Nema and the Nemettes." And with that, Nema flicked her hair and flounced off again.

"Aarrgghh, that is so, so…" Emma couldn't find the words.

"So Nema," suggested Hannah.

"Exactly," laughed Emma. "Come on, guys, let's do our band practice."

"Her band should be called Nema and the Nasties," suggested Elle, as they walked into the music room for their practice.

"Yes! Or how about Nema and the Hair Flickers?" said Isi, giggling.

Once in the music room, the girls quickly got their instruments set up and were soon ready to play.

"So, what song should we play?" asked Hannah.

"How about 'Rock 'n' Shine,'" suggested Elle. "We all love that one, don't we?"

Everyone agreed and the girls began to play. Isi began with the really solid drumbeat that started the song, and then Hannah joined in on bass guitar, building on the beat, holding the song together, solidly in the background. Just like Hannah, really. Elle came in next on keyboard, often adding new bits as she went along. Finally, Emma started in on lead guitar with the song tune. The girls all turned and smiled at each other as they played. It was such a buzz how the music all came together. They listened to each other and let each instrument and girl do its thing. Together they were fabulous. They played the song through to the end almost perfectly.

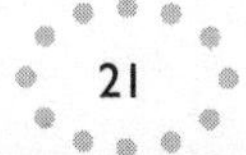

"That was great," said Isi. "Who do you think should sing this one?"

"Emma," said Elle. "She has the best voice for this song."

"Oh no, I don't think so, Elle," said Emma. "You do it. You're the best performer by far."

"No, Elle's right, Em," said Hannah. "You should sing it. It's your favorite song and it seems just perfect for you."

Emma gulped. Things were getting worse. Now she wasn't just performing, her friends wanted her to be the lead singer. It was true she loved the song, but that was singing it into her hairbrush, not on stage. Emma didn't think she could do that. It would be like the kindergarten concert all over again. She wouldn't shine, she would just be hopelessly shy and mess everything up. And ruin her friends' chance in the competition. Emma felt her eyes starting to sting. Again. *Gee whizz, lemonfizz, this is getting embarrassing,* thought Emma.

Piinngg!

Saved by the phone! It was a mission alert from

SHINE.

"Hey, I have to go," said Emma looking up from her phone, "but don't wait for me. I may be a while."

Emma's friends just smiled at Emma and at each other—they were used to her suddenly leaving. It was just one of those things that happened when your friend was a secret agent.

Chapter 3

Emma headed toward the girls' bathroom. She had already been there once this lunchtime and hoped no one would notice that she was going again. She didn't want anyone to get suspicious. Outside the bathroom Nema and her friends were playing jump rope. They had been there all lunchtime. Emma was hoping she could just slip by without them noticing, without them commenting. She couldn't.

"Hey, weren't you just here?" said Nema.

"Oh, right, you know, I have to go to the bathroom," mumbled Emma.

"But you've just been," said Nema. "Got a problem?" Nema seemed to like it when people had problems.

Yes, you, thought Emma, but instead answered, "Well, you know, I have drunk a lot of water, a *lot* of water. It's really good for you, water, you should try it, Nema," as she was really, really wishing that her missions didn't have to start in the girls' bathroom.

But they did. **SHINE** needed reliable access points for their Mission Tube. The Mission Tube was a secret transportation system, a network of underground tunnels that carried agents to **SHINE HQ** and other locations. The access points had to be somewhere that the agent often went and somewhere that it would be reasonable and easy to go to without attracting attention. When you thought about it like that, the girls' bathroom at Emma's school made perfect sense—but it didn't make it any less embarrassing.

Emma walked into the bathroom and checked to see if there was anyone else there. There wasn't, thank goodness. With the room clear, she headed for the last

stall on the right and pushed the door open. She went in and locked the door. Emma put down the toilet seat, and sat down and flipped open the toilet paper holder. There, if you knew what to look for, was, besides toilet paper, the SHINE Mission Tube access socket. Emma pushed her phone into the socket and waited. There was a beep, then Emma entered her pin code and removed her phone. Another beep and then the usual message flashed up on her phone screen.

WELCOME BACK EJ12.
HOLD ON!

The wall behind the toilet spun around, with the toilet and EJ12 still attached. The toilet then tipped slightly and EJ slipped off the toilet seat and onto a beanbag at the top of what looked like a giant tunnel slide. A protective shield came over the back of the beanbag, covering EJ. The wall then spun back and EJ could hear the click as the stall door unlocked on the other side. A locked stall with no one inside would raise suspicions and SHINE didn't want that. On her side of the wall, EJ was ready, she keyed "go" into her phone and...

WHOOOOOOOOOSH

EJ traveled down the tube that led away from her school and into the SHINE tube network, whizzing around corners at high speed. As she traveled, EJ could hear music piped through the Mission Tube. *That's new, nice touch,* she thought. Soon, however, just in the middle of one of her favorite songs, EJ came to a stop at a small platform with a keypad and screen. The protective shield over the beanbag flipped back and EJ again entered her pin code on the keypad and waited. The security check was about to commence.

The check changed each time. Sometimes it was an eye scan, sometimes voice recognition. It was different every time to prevent anyone breaking into the SHINE network.

"Please sign your autograph on the screen pad," requested a digital voice.

Cool! thought Emma, as she signed her name on the screen. Emma liked signing her name and was always trying to write it in a new style. This time, however, she decided she'd better write normally.

Emma Jacks

There was a short, sharp flash.

"Handwriting check complete. Handwriting quite messy, but agent identity confirmed. Please drop in, EJ12!"

There was another beep as the platform beneath her opened up and EJ, still on her beanbag, dropped gently down into the Code Room. There was nothing in the room but a table, a chair and a clear plastic tube protruding from the ceiling. **SHINE** liked their tubes. EJ moved to the chair and waited. She heard the familiar whizzing noise, put her hands out under the tube and caught a little capsule that popped out of it. EJ opened the capsule and took out a small piece of paper and a pen. It was an intercepted code and Emma read it.

For EJ12's eyes only.

Message intercepted from SHADOW 13.23.

Sent to EJ12 13.31.

Urgent decode required.

7-4-6-5 7-4-2-3-6-9-7

2-6-6-2-3-7-8 2-6-4-8-3.

2-8-9 4-2-4-7 2-6-3 4-3-2-3-7-3-8.

The first thing that caught EJ's attention was the picture of the mobile phone. That had to mean something, but what? Then she noticed something else about the message: there was no number higher than nine. That had to tell her something too. Hmmm. EJ took out her phone and as soon as she saw the keypad, something clicked in her mind.

EJ was now pretty sure she knew how to crack the code.

It's a mobile text code, she thought. *If I match the numbers to the ones on the phone keypad, I think I will get words, just like a text message. Let's test it.* EJ keyed the first set of numbers into her phone. As she did, the letters appeared on her screen and EJ wrote them down under the coded message.

7-4-6-5
PINK

Then the next set.

7-4-2-3-6-9-7
SHADOWS

Pink Shadows? The band, Pink Shadows? Why were they in the message? What did they have to do with a **SHINE** *Mission? Did they have something to do with the* **SHADOW** *agency? Surely not,* thought EJ, as she moved on to the next set of numbers.

2-6-6-2-3-7-8
CONCEPT

Concept? Could that be right? It didn't feel right. Could it be another word? EJ pressed the predictive text for more options. *That's better,* she thought, when she saw the next option appear.

CONCERT

EJ quickly keyed in the remaining number sets then wrote the decoded message under the code.

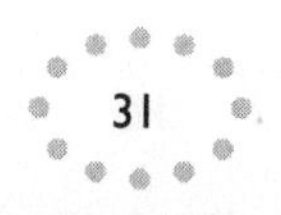

7-4-6-5 7-4-2-3-6-9-7
PINK SHADOWS
2-6-6-2-3-7-8 2-6-4-8-3.
CONCERT 2NITE.
2-8-9 4-2-4-7 2-6-3 4-3-2-3-7-3-8.
BUY HAIR AND HEADSET.

EJ looked at the now decoded message but could hardly believe what she was reading. *The Pink Shadows concert? Is this really an intercepted message from **SHADOW**?* thought EJ. EJ looked at the message again. It was not like any message she had ever decoded before. It was more like a message that a friend would send to another friend. *Had **SHINE** made a mistake?* wondered EJ.

EJ was still trying to work out what the message might mean as she rolled up the paper with the decoded message, put it back in the capsule and then slipped the capsule up the tube. There was a whoosh as the capsule was sucked up and away toward **SHINE HQ** where the head of **SHINE**, A1, would be waiting for it—and for EJ12. Perhaps with A1's help she would be able to work out what the message meant. EJ hoped so.

Chapter 4

EJ had reentered the Mission Tube and, after a short trip, arrived at her next stop. Large metal doors slid apart and EJ walked into the Operations Room of SHINE HQ. EJ was pleased to see that things were back to normal with lights on and computer screens flashing. It wasn't so long ago that SHINE's energy supplies had been attacked by *SHADOW*. SHINE had been reduced to using emergency lighting and candles. It was, as she proudly remembered, EJ who had worked out what *SHADOW* was doing and stopped them from blacking out SHINE permanently.

"Hello again, EJ12," said A1, "welcome back. I hope you had a nice trip. Did you enjoy our new in-tube music?"

A1 was the head of the **SHINE** agency and she was responsible for briefing agents for their missions. A1 was, as always, wearing a smart black suit with a white shirt and a long silver chain with a beautiful, almost glowing, yellow pendant. A1's long white hair was swooped up in a rather messy bun held with a tortoiseshell comb at the back. There could be all sorts of things sticking out of the bun, but today, EJ noticed, there was just a pencil.

"As you can see, EJ, we are back to normal and have full power again, but we have introduced some energy-saving devices as a result of that last mishap. Remember one of our favorite mottoes, 'If you get lemons, you can make lemonade'; there is always something good that can come from bad things."

EJ nodded, wondering if there was anything that **SHINE** did not have a motto for.

"We have a motto for most things, EJ12," said A1, who always seemed to know what EJ was thinking,

which was a bit disconcerting. "Do you know," she continued, "that this is one of the first SHADOW messages that we have intercepted in quite some time? We simply have not been able to find them. They could be planning something big and we don't know anything. But now, thank goodness, we have this message. We had been keeping an eye on a particular SHADOW agent and managed to intercept the message from SHADOW that was sent to her phone. We made a copy of the message before sending it on to the agent. She shouldn't suspect anything and SHADOW won't know that we might be on to them. Now, let's look at that message." A1 turned toward the screen. "Light Screen, lower. Show message."

On A1's command, an enormous screen came down from the ceiling. It was the Light Screen, a giant, voice-activated plasma screen that accessed the Internet, all SHINE's classified files, radio and television channels and GPS technology too. You could also use it as a touch screen and move pictures around, grouping things together. It was very clever and very cool. The decoded message that EJ had just cracked flashed onto the screen.

> Message intercepted from SHADOW 13.23.
> Sent to EJ12 13.31.
> Decoded message received at SHINE 13.52.
> Time taken to decode 0.21.
>
> 7-4-6-5 7-4-2-3-6-9-7
> PINK SHADOWS
> 2-6-6-2-3-7-8 2-6-4-8-3.
> CONCERT 2NITE.
> 2-8-9 4-2-4-7 2-6-3 4-3-2-3-7-3-8.
> BUY HAIR AND HEADSET.

EJ looked at the bit that said how long it took to crack the code. "That's new," said EJ, frowning. She loved cracking codes, but she didn't like timed tests.

"Yes, that's right,, EJ. We need to keep track of our agents' times and make sure they are improving. Don't look so worried, you did well, EJ," said

A1, smiling. "Now I think this message is very interesting. I have been hearing a lot about the Pink Shadows lately."

"They are one of the hottest bands around," said EJ, wondering if A1 kept up with new music—she wouldn't be surprised.

"Yes, I suspect you are not surprised that I know that. Indeed I received an email with a free download to one of their songs the other day, although I must say I haven't gotten around to doing it yet. I think it is a re-max."

"A remix?" asked EJ helpfully, trying not to giggle.

"Yes, that was it, a remix," said A1. "How did you know?"

"That's the word for a new version of a song," explained EJ.

"Oh, is it? Well that's a new word for me, thanks, EJ. Now let's see what we know about these Pink Shadows people." A1 turned back to the Light Screen and said, "Pink Shadows. Show data, show footage."

Images started to flood the Light Screen, of the band, of the lead singer, Shady Lady, of the band

at awards ceremonies. Videos started streaming of music clips, interviews and concert performances.

"Goodness, there is a lot. Report summary," said A1.

A digital voice began talking. "The Pink Shadows is one of the most popular bands in the world. They release a new song every month and their songs always hit the top ten and are some of the most popular downloads. Their recent hits include 'Listen Up,' 'Master Plan' and 'Getting Dark.' Their latest song is 'Rock 'n' Shine.' The band tours constantly. They are currently on their fourth tour across the country, the Decoder Tour. Shady Lady is the band's new lead singer and is known for her unusual and striking stage costumes as well as her wild stage performances. There have been rumors that the other band members are tiring of Shady Lady already, saying she is always overshadowing them, but this is not confirmed. She is rarely seen without her dog, Pinky-poo, who, to animal rights groups' concern, is dressed in clothes and kept in Shady Lady's handbag. Although small, Pinky-poo has been known to bite journalists who ask difficult questions. The Pink Shadows are playing the final concert of the Decoder Tour tonight to a sold-out stadium. There is a lot of online chat about the rumor that they may release a new version of 'Rock 'n' Shine,' but this has not been confirmed. End of summary."

"Pink *Shadows, Decoder* Tour, is that just a coincidence?" asked A1. "I am not at all sure. And there is something else that is making me extremely suspicious. Watch this, EJ," said A1, as she again turned back to the screen. "Show Pink Shadows tour dates and locations."

A string of dates appeared.

"Show tracked ***SHADOW*** Internet activity, by date," said A1, who then turned back to EJ. "While we haven't been able to find out what they are doing, we have been able to track their Internet usage. And what we have discovered from that is interesting, very interesting indeed. Look."

Another string of data appeared on the screen.

"Cross reference," said A1.

As EJ watched, the two sets of data were merged into each other.

"Do you see the pattern, EJ?" asked A1.

"Yes!"

"Well, what is it?" asked A1.

"Oh right, sorry," said EJ, quickly continuing. "There is a big increase in **SHADOW** Internet activity the day after a Pink Shadows concert. Actually, there is a big increase in **SHADOW** Internet activity the day after *every* Pink Shadows concert."

"Exactly," said A1. "Another coincidence? I don't think so. And now, in this message, **SHADOW** is telling its agent to go to the Pink Shadows concert, here, tonight. The question is why? Will there be more Internet activity after this concert as well? What will the agent do at a rock music concert and why will she need to buy hair and headset? What does 'hair and headset' even mean? Will there be more than one **SHADOW** agent there? There are so many questions and we need to find out the answers. And quickly. I am afraid you are going to have to go to that concert, EJ12."

Is she kidding? thought EJ. *Who wouldn't want to go to a Pink Shadows concert?*

"Okay, I'm ready, A1," replied EJ smiling. "I think I can cope."

Chapter 5

EJ12's mission gear was laid out, as usual, on the briefing table, but it was pretty unusual gear. Rather than binoculars there were heart-shaped sunglasses, rather than a backpack there was a nifty denim shoulder bag with lots of little buttons pinned to it. There were buttons with pictures of puppies, a baby monkey, even a button that said "I ♥ Penguins" and another saying "100% math." It was as if it had been all created especially for EJ. Instead of cargo pants and a standard-issue mission T-shirt, there was a pair of faded jeans and, EJ's eyes lit up when she saw

it, a limited edition Pink Shadows tour T-shirt. There was also a black leather jacket and a pair of indigo-colored sneakers that looked to be exactly EJ's size.

"The sneakers can also become platform sneakers, EJ. If you need a bit more height, simply click and wait for the heels to extend. They may help you look for things in the crowd. You will also be needing this," said A1, as she passed EJ her concert ticket. "There is a wallet in your bag with some money in it. Keep the ticket there so you don't lose it."

A1 sounded just like EJ's mom. She often did, but EJ didn't mind, it was good to know that someone was looking out for you. Before she put it away, EJ looked at the ticket and gasped. It wasn't just any concert ticket, it was a ticket for Pink Class, the best section in the stadium.

"How did you get this?" asked EJ. "These tickets have been sold out for months."

"Oh, we have our ways," said A1, smiling. "You may need this as well," said A1, giving EJ a plastic disk, attached to a long pink cord. "It is a backstage pass. Put it around your neck and if anyone asks,

tell them you won it in a 'Light Up Your Life' radio competition. Now, EJ, this is another night mission. Are you ready for that?"

"Absolutely, A1," replied EJ without hesitating. "You could say that I have seen the light on being scared of the dark!"

"Well done, EJ12," said A1. "And I do like a word joke. In fact, that reminds me of another SHINE motto: 'It's always more fun when you use a good pun.'"

EJ groaned at that one, then spied an mp3 player on the briefing table. It had a metallic indigo cover which, along with aqua, was one of EJ's favorite colors. It looked slightly different from the ones in stores.

"This is a special SHINE-issue mp3 player, EJ. It's a spy-pod and has extra functions including a record function. There is also a SHINE-issue headset, but make sure you buy another at the concert, as the message instructed. And some hair, whatever that means. Okay, let's move on to your new charms."

CHARM stood for Clever Hidden Accessories with Release Mechanism. The SHINE inventors were always creating new devices for their agents. They invented baby penguin food dispensers, glow-in-the-dark string, spray to attract butterflies and spray to repel spiders, but their cleverest invention was a method to shrink all this equipment and hide it within charms. The agent simply wore the charm bracelet on her wrist and, when she needed to, activated the device by twisting the charm. It worked, as A1 liked to say, like a charm! Depending on where the agent was going and what she might need to do, the SHINE inventors would create new charms.

EJ saw that there were four new silver charms laid out on the briefing table. There was a little microphone, a dog bone, a guitar and a heart with musical notes engraved on it.

"I really think we have outdone ourselves this time," said A1. "Look at the microphone charm, EJ. This charm is embedded with SHINE-created micro-speak technology. Once activated, you simply select your voice type and then speak into the

microphone. Your voice will be disguised as the selected voice. You can sound like a young man, an old woman, a small child; there is quite a range to choose from, including animal noises. It is quite ingenious, even if we do say so ourselves. You can also pick your language—once you talk into it, it will translate and, *voila*! It will produce the words in that language. And last, but by no means least, if you use your spy-pod to record a voice, you can connect it up and micro-speak will be able to copy it, allowing you to sound exactly like that person. It could be very useful to get past voice-recognition tests."

"Wow," said EJ, "that is amazing." *And*, she thought, *imagine what I could do with it to annoy Bob.*

"Just remember, EJ," said A1 frowning slightly, "the charms cannot be used outside missions."

"Oh, of course not," said EJ, blushing. She thought she'd better move the conversation on. "What does this little dog bone do, A1?"

"I am glad you asked," said A1. "It's our new dog-whisperer charm. We are a little bit worried about

Shady Lady's dog, Pinky-poo. She seems rather temperamental. If she does give you any trouble, this charm will help you manage her."

That is so cool, thought EJ. *I wish you could use them out of missions—it might work on Nema.*

"Okay, EJ12, the concert stadium is out of town and we need to get you there well before the show starts so you can have a look around. We must not miss a beat. There will be a further briefing once you are on your way. Now you need to get changed and prepare yourself for departure," said A1.

EJ headed off to the dressing room with her clothes. SHINE always got the right size and EJ felt confident and ready for anything once she changed into her mission gear, even if it was jeans and a leather jacket this time. Her school uniform would be washed and sent home to EJ's mom who, being a former SHINE agent herself, wouldn't be surprised. Actually she would be thrilled that someone else had washed the uniform for a change.

Dressed and feeling fabulous, EJ attached her charms to her bracelet, put her backstage pass around her neck and packed her spy-pod, headset, wallet and phone into her shoulder bag. Then she heard A1's voice over the intercom.

"EJ12, push the button to the right of the dressing room door and you can exit directly to the SHINE underground parking lot, where your limousine is waiting for you. Good luck and keep in contact."

A limo? Could this mission get any better? EJ12 was ready to rock.

Chapter 6

EJ sat in the back of the most enormous car she had ever seen, let alone been in. The glass panel between the back and front of the car slid aside and the driver looked at EJ through the rearview mirror.

"Hello, EJ12, and welcome. I am Agent REV1, your driver today. You are sitting in a SHINE hybrid-powered limousine, one of the first in the world. Incredibly quiet, very environmentally friendly and glamorous, it has everything you might need or want. Make yourself comfortable, help yourself to a drink and then tune into the in-car television for a mission briefing."

"Thanks, Agent REV1," said EJ, "I'll do that."

Make myself comfortable, thought EJ, *that shouldn't be hard!*

EJ was sitting on a white leather sofa, which curved around in a semicircle. On the floor was white fluffy carpet and in front of the sofa was a large television with enormous speakers on either side. There was also a cabinet with rows of glasses next to a small fridge stocked with delicious fruit juices and soft drinks and a freezer full of ice cream.

EJ leaned forward and made herself a raspberry lemonade in a long glass. As a finishing touch, she added a little paper umbrella and a straw and sat back, smiling. This was so cool and there was so much room. All the members of Squishy Music could have fit, and she wished Hannah, Elle and Isi were there to share this. They would have loved the rock star treatment.

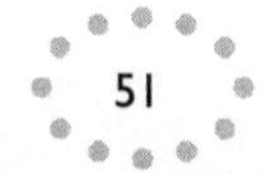

EJ turned on the television. The **SHINE** logo appeared with a menu below.

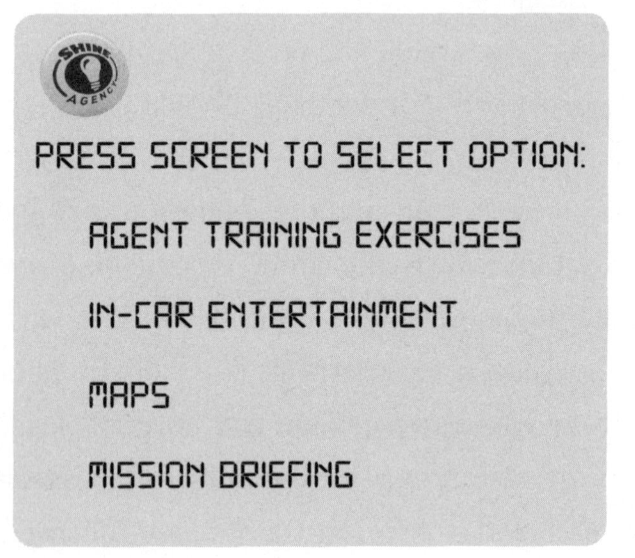

Training exercises, that sounds like homework, thought EJ, as she pressed "Mission Briefing" and A1 appeared on the screen.

"Hello again, EJ12. I trust you are finding your drive comfortable," said A1. "Now let's review your mission objectives. We are pretty sure that ***SHADOW*** is planning something and we suspect that that something is somehow connected to both the Internet and the Pink Shadows concerts. Your job, EJ12, is to find what the something and what the somehow is.

"To help you, the in-car entertainment system has been loaded with material about the Pink Shadows and, in particular, Shady Lady. The connection between **SHADOW** Internet activity and the Pink Shadows concerts only started when she joined the band. Do review these, EJ12. They may give us some more clues.

"Please also check your equipment. While your phone is also an mp3 player, the spy-pod has enhanced audio options, particularly our new hyper-hear listening device.

"You will also need the spy-pod if you wish to use your guitar charm, EJ," continued A1. "Once activated, clip the charm to the spy-pod and upload required songs. You can then clip the charm to the fret of any electric or acoustic guitar and select a music track. The charm will then 'play' the selected song. All you need to do is pretend that you are playing and the charm will do the rest. Okay, EJ12, that's all. Make contact when you find out what's going on. Good luck. SHINE out."

EJ took another sip of her drink then returned to the menu on the touch screen and pressed "In-car Entertainment." She could then select the program she wanted to view. EJ chose an interview with Shady Lady and sat back and watched.

The Music Now music channel logo appeared and then cut to Shady Lady sitting on a black leather sofa. For someone who seemed larger than life, Shady Lady was actually tiny, hardly taller than EJ. But what she lacked in height, she made up for in her outfits. For this interview, she was wearing bright-pink tights, pink boots and what looked like a long, sleeveless, pink raincoat decorated with black dots. On her wrists and forearms she was wearing dozens of black and pink bangles and she had a tattoo on her upper right arm of a black heart with a treble clef shooting through it like a lightning bolt. She looked amazing, in a crazy, rock star kind of way. Pinky-poo was next to her, also wearing a little pink raincoat, and was sitting in Shady Lady's handbag again. *Poor dog*, thought EJ. *No wonder she bites. I think I would probably bite if I was being dressed up like that and squashed in a handbag all the time.*

A woman was sitting opposite Shady Lady and now she leaned forward toward the singer with her microphone and began to ask questions.

"You've made quite an impact on the Pink Shadows since you joined the band earlier this year," started the interviewer. "How are you settling in?"

"I'm like totally having a blast," replied Shady Lady.

"Your song lyrics are wild, Shady, so imaginative, they're almost like a secret code. Where do you get your inspiration from?" she asked.

"Well, you know, it's like, I just kind of feel it, and it comes together out of the shadows and into my head, into my music."

"Okay," said the interviewer, looking a little confused. "Your live shows are amazing. How does it feel to be on stage?"

"I love performing, it's so totally my life, you know," said Shady Lady. "I can, like, connect with my

Shadow peeps, take my message to them."

"Is there any truth to the rumors that the other band members feel you are taking over, sending a different message than the one they want?"

EJ noticed that Shady Lady suddenly looked less relaxed, even a bit scary. The singer sat up in her chair and her eyes narrowed.

"No," she said sharply, glaring at the interviewer. "Next question."

"And what can the fans expect from the Decoder Tour?" asked the interviewer, a little nervously.

Shady Lady lounged back on the chair, at ease again. "It's, like, our best yet. It's like totally sick. Everyone will be racing to upload our songs. And for our last song at our last gig, we'll play a brand-new, never before heard remix of 'Rock 'n' Shine.' I guarantee you," said Shady Lady, turning to face the camera with a not completely friendly gleam in her eye, "it will be chaos!"

"Thanks, Shady Lady, I think," said the interviewer, turning to face the camera. "Now let's take a look at the Pink Shadows, live in concert at one of their earlier shows."

EJ watched, entranced. The concert was amazing, especially Shady Lady who danced and leapt all over the stage, dazzling the audience. She even sang one song hanging upside down from a trapeze.

Shady Lady certainly doesn't have a problem with stage fright, thought EJ, as her mind wandered back to her own band and the We've Got Talent competition. Thinking about it again made her feel nervous, nervous about performing, nervous about letting her friends down. Her friends, that reminded EJ, she needed to upload her mission BESTie.

SHINE understood that no agent could do everything by herself and that everyone needed help—with knowledge, guidance or sometimes just moral support. BEST stood for Brains, Expertise, Support, Tips and every agent had a network of people she could call on to help her. The BESTies, as they were known, were screened by **SHINE HQ** and cleared to help the agent on missions. Sometimes they helped with codes, sometimes they had expert information, but more often they were there to support the agent when the mission got tough. The BESTies could ask no questions and an agent could never discuss her work with them when a mission was over. And there was another rule—an agent could only choose one BESTie for each mission.

Who will be able to help me on this mission? wondered EJ, twisting her bracelet absentmindedly. She flicked through her contacts, Elle, Hannah, Isi, Mom…EJ thought back to when she and Elle were singing and dancing at her house. All of EJ's BESTies were great to have as backup, but they each had different things they were good at. EJ tried to think. Who would be the best BESTie for this mission? There seemed to be a lot about music in this mission and that made EJ think Elle could be a good choice. Elle knew all the words, all the dance moves, everything about the Pink Shadows—and she always got EJ up and dancing, made her feel good. EJ uploaded Elle, who would now be sent a text message alerting her to be on standby for mission assist.

Agent REV1 slid back the window again. "We are

approaching the stadium now, EJ12. Are you ready?"

Ready for what? wondered EJ. She would have to be ready for anything. It was showtime!

Chapter 7

The white limousine cruised into the stadium parking lot and past the crowds lining up to get in. As a Pink Class ticket-holder, EJ had premium parking and could drive straight through. When the car stopped, a doorman opened the car door for EJ.

"Welcome to Pink Class, miss," said the doorman. "Please follow the pink carpet to enter the stadium. Don't forget to pick up your exclusive merchandise in the foyer, and enjoy the show."

EJ was excited. She felt like a rock star. *But this is still a mission and I have to keep focused,* she told herself. *I need to check out the stadium and I need to buy my headset. And my hair, whatever that means!*

EJ walked down the pink carpet and followed the signs to the stadium foyer. EJ had never been to a concert before and was thrilled by the buzz of the crowd. It was hard to see though. EJ clicked her sneakers and waited. Within seconds she was about a foot taller and could see everything. *I wouldn't walk in these, though,* thought EJ. *It would be impossible!*

There were people milling around stands where you could buy Pink Shadows T-shirts, glasses, posters, books, even Pink Shadows pajamas. There were food and drink counters and people everywhere, excited people, thousands of Pink Shadows fans, many in pink and many wearing shiny fluorescent-pink wigs made of strips of pink foil. It really was crazy hair. Then EJ remembered the message. *Hair. Buy Hair. I can't believe I am saying this, but I need that hair,* thought EJ. She looked around and then saw a stand and a sign.

Crazy Shady Lady Pink Hair

EJ headed over to buy her crazy hair, although how it was going to help her she had no idea.

How many ***SHADOW*** *agents are here?* wondered EJ, as she paid for the hair. There was certainly one, the one whose message SHINE had intercepted, but were there more? Was everyone wearing pink hair a ***SHADOW*** agent? EJ began looking at different people, trying to guess if any of them were agents. She couldn't though; ***SHADOW*** would make sure their agents blended in, just like SHINE did. But if they were here, they would do something and EJ needed to be ready.

Suddenly an announcement blared through the stadium foyer.

"Please take your seats. The Pink Shadows concert will begin in five minutes."

I'd better hurry up, thought EJ and she quickly bought a pink glow stick and a headset. She took a quick look at it, but the headset looked pretty much like any other, besides being very pink. Could it really be part of a **SHADOW** plan? EJ stuffed it and the pink hair into her bag and made her way to the Pink Class section at the very front of the stage area. She checked her ticket for her seat number. It was AA 24, front row. Awesome!

EJ had just found her seat when the stadium went completely dark, except for the sea of pink glow sticks being waved all around her. EJ waved hers too. Then the crowd suddenly hushed. Everyone was waiting.

A single pink laser began to flash across the stage. Then another laser flashed and then another. Lasers started to appear everywhere, flashing around the stadium and over the heads of the audience, who were now cheering wildly. Then, as suddenly as they started, the lasers stopped and everything went

dark again. As a single drumbeat echoed around the stadium, a screen at the back of the stage turned bright neon-pink and then began to flash in time with the drumbeat. Next, four dark figures were slowly lowered from the top of the stadium. They came down to the stage, black silhouettes in front of the pink screen, silhouettes of four women, one on drums, one with a bass guitar, one on keyboard and one with a lead guitar and a microphone stand. Suddenly the screen went black and the silhouettes turned pink—pink shadows, the Pink Shadows. Jets of pink smoke started to stream up from the stage as the drumbeat quickened and the neon-pink screen flashed faster. A voice boomed through the stadium.

"Live, on the final night of their Decoder Tour, the Pink Shadows!"

The stage lights went on and the band started to play. The whole crowd went completely crazy, screaming and stamping their feet. EJ joined in, feeling herself pulled into the incredible atmosphere. It was exhilarating. And leading it all, in the center of the stage, was Shady Lady. She was wearing a pink jumpsuit, glittering with hundreds of silver flecks and knee-high, almost impossibly high-heeled silver boots. She was wearing a straight black wig and her face was completely white, like a Japanese doll. Black-line makeup swirled around her face, like a painting of black ivy trailing her eyes. She looked awesome, a bit scary but awesome. The makeup was like a mask on her face.

Shady Lady walked down the catwalk that came out from the center of the stage, prowling, stalking her way down until she was standing almost in the middle of the crowd. Then she raised one arm above her head and pointed upward. There was a flash and the stadium went dark again except for a pink light beam shooting out from a large black ring on Shady Lady's finger. The crowd roared and the lights went on as Shady Lady brought her arm down again and started to play her guitar. Then beams of light shot out from rings each of the band members was wearing and they began to play their chart hit, "Getting Dark."

EJ looked around the crowd, trying to detect

anything unusual, but she couldn't. There were just lots of people enjoying the show, cheering, screaming and dancing to the songs. Perhaps SHINE had been wrong about the message?

The Pink Shadows had been playing for nearly an hour when Shady Lady shouted out, "Okay, do we have any Shadows out there?"

There was a roar from the crowd.

EJ started. *Did she say Shadows? Did she mean Pink Shadows or Shadows, SHADOW agents? Maybe there is something going on after all.*

Shady Lady went on. "Oh yeah, we do I guess. Well I'm talking to you, all you Shadows. Get your heads pink, the song after this is for you!"

EJ turned around and scanned the crowd again. This time, there was something suspicious happening. Suddenly people seemed to be putting on the pink headsets. As the Pink Shadows started to play the song, EJ did the same, plugging it into her spy-pod. Where else would she plug it? Not surprisingly, she couldn't hear anything through the headset.

Maybe mine is broken, she thought, but as she looked around her, she could see other people doing the same thing, taking off their headsets, shaking their mp3 players and looking irritated. *They can't all be broken, can they?* Then, still watching the crowd, she noticed something else. Some other people were still wearing their headsets and everyone who was seemed to be wearing a crazy Shady Lady pink hair wig. A coincidence? EJ checked out different parts of the stadium and yes, everyone still with their headsets on had pink hair.

The song finished and then Shady Lady cried out, "Okay, Shadow peeps, hold on to your hair, this is it, rock on!"

Hair. Suddenly things started to make sense to EJ. Shadow peeps, hair, all the people still using the headsets wearing the Shady Lady hair. It had to be connected but how? Were all the people wearing crazy hair ***SHADOW*** agents? Did you need to use both the hair and the headset at the same time? EJ wasn't sure, but there was only one way to find out.

She grabbed her wig and as she held it upside down to put it on she noticed the label.

Headset Hair.

Another crazy idea from Shadow Inc.

Headset Hair? What did that mean? EJ looked closely at the wig and lifted the label. There was nothing there. Or was there . . . EJ looked again, even more closely than before and this time she could see something. A tiny hole. A little hole to connect a headset to? No one would look there and no one would think twice about a little hole—unless of course, they knew what they were looking for. EJ took the headset and put the plug into the hole. It fit perfectly, just as EJ suspected it would. *You had to hand it to* **SHADOW**, thought EJ, *they did come up with some clever, if a bit crazy, ideas.* She wondered if Adriana X, A1's evil twin sister, was behind the crazy hair.

With the headset connected, EJ put her earphones in and put on the pink hair. The wig fit perfectly over the headset and she could feel them lock into each other. There was a beep and then, just as the next song was starting, EJ started to hear things. But what she heard wasn't what she was expecting. Things were starting to get interesting.

The Pink Shadows were really knocking out the song on stage. Shady Lady was now swinging over the audience from a rope suspended from the stadium roof.

With the headset off, the noise of the concert was almost deafening, but with the headset on EJ heard something very unexpected. She could still hear the music, but now more as a fuzzy background noise, almost a buzz. The headset hair seemed to be blocking out all the noise, the band, the crowd, everything except Shady Lady's singing. And, as

EJ listened, she noticed something. Shady Lady was singing a different chorus from the usual version. As well as the words she knew, there seemed to be other, new words added to the chorus, a new one every ten seconds or so. And the headset made these words louder. But why? As the song was coming up to the chorus again, EJ connected her spy-pod to the headset and set it to record. There were the same new words again in the chorus.

The song finished and the Pink Shadows left the stage. It was intermission and the perfect time for EJ to try to work out if those extra words were connected to ***SHADOW***. EJ needed a place where she could be alone, where she could play back the chorus, but where could you find a place like that at a sold-out rock concert?

"Oh no," she said to herself, as she thought of somewhere, "not again."

The bathroom. The only place EJ could think of was the bathroom. Why was she always finding herself sitting on a toilet seat as part of a top secret mission, and just when she thought this mission

was more glamorous?

EJ made her way toward the bathroom, but she wasn't the only one. In fact, it seemed like the entire audience was heading in the same direction and as EJ got closer she could see a long line outside the women's bathroom. So much for that idea, but where could she go? Then EJ spied a door with a sign saying "Cleaners only." EJ tried the door, but it was locked. EJ took her key charm and twisted it to activate the skeleton key. Quickly, hoping no one would see, EJ unlocked the door and stepped inside. Actually outside. EJ was standing outside in a dimly lit, very smelly area with all the trash cans from the food stands.

Guess I was wrong, thought EJ, *there is somewhere less glamorous than the bathroom after all.* But it was quiet and she was all alone, which is exactly what she needed.

EJ took out her spy-pod, switched it to playback and listened. As the song, or at least what was left of it, played back through EJ's headphones, she took out her phone, scrolled to the notepad app and keyed in the extra words from the chorus she heard.

Song, False, To, Last, Up, Code,
Load, In, Note

That doesn't mean anything at all! thought EJ, crinkling up her nose and looking at what she had written. Perhaps the headset was just broken after all. But then EJ thought back to the Shady Lady interview she had watched in the limo and to something the interviewer had said. She had said that the Pink Shadows song lyrics were "like a code." Perhaps they weren't like a code, perhaps they *were* a code. A code EJ needed to crack. She looked at the words again and, with a pen and paper began moving the words around, rearranging them to see if she could get them to make sense.

False Song In Code To Last Up Load Note

False Song? Was that something? False Song in code? But what was a false song? EJ tried again.

Note To Last Song False Up Load Code In

Was it something about the Last Song? wondered EJ. *That made more sense than a False Song,* she thought. *And, hold on, Up Load Code, that had to mean something, but what?*

Nothing seemed to make sense. At least some words looked like they might mean something, but not the whole sentence. EJ was sure that these words, in the right order, did mean something, something to do with ***SHADOW***. EJ tried another word order.

Up Load Last Song To False Note In Code

"Hmm, is that it?" said EJ to herself. Upload the last song? Maybe that made sense, but the rest of the sentence didn't seem to mean anything. Or did it? Was False Note something? Was it something in code? EJ felt all the possibilities were now just whirring around in her head, but she kept going. EJ tried another word order.

Up Load Code To Last Song In False Note

EJ looked at what she had written and then smiled to herself. "That's not right, but now I am pretty sure I know what is," she said, as she quickly scribbled it down, afraid it might fly out of her head.

Up Load Code To False Note In Last Song

Up Load Code. *Yes,* thought EJ. *I am pretty sure the message is talking about an upload code. That would explain* ***SHADOW's*** *Internet activity, they are uploading codes. And that upload code could be in the last song, the last song of something. Maybe it means the last song of the Pink Shadows concert.*

That could make sense, EJ decided, but she still didn't understand what False Note was. She was, however, pretty sure she had the right word order and that the message was a code from **SHADOW**. And, that could only mean one thing—Shady Lady had to be connected to **SHADOW**. *She was singing the message so she just had to be, didn't she?*

thought EJ, her mind spinning with what that meant.

A1 was right. It is all too much of a coincidence, thought EJ. *How could we not have picked it up? The Pink* ***Shadows****, how could we not have gotten that? And* ***Shady*** *Lady? Of course, ugh, it's so obvious—once you know.*

EJ again thought back to the interview. What else had Shady Lady said? She had said that she was taking a message to her Shadow peeps. Now it began to make sense to EJ. Could it be that Shady Lady really was "taking a message," a code, to her peeps and that her peeps were ***SHADOW*** agents? The Decoder Tour—that was how ***SHADOW*** had been communicating with their agents, through the songs! Shady Lady had been hiding the messages in the songs and the agents had been using the headset hair to decode it. Who would ever have suspected crazy pink hair would be the key to a secret message system? Then again, who would have thought that Shady Lady was a ***SHADOW*** agent? She had to be, but were the other band members involved too?

With a sudden chill, EJ remembered what else

Shady Lady had said. "And for our last song at our last gig, we will play a brand-new, never before heard remix of 'Rock 'n' Shine.' It will be chaos!"

EJ needed to call A1 to tell her what she had found out. She took out her phone and called. A1 answered immediately.

"EJ12, what is your report?" asked A1.

"Shady Lady works, as you suspected, for ***SHADOW***. I'm not sure about the rest of the band."

"I thought so," said A1. "I never did like the way she treated her dog. That should have been another clue. What else did you find out?"

"She has been sending messages to ***SHADOW*** agents via their songs and I think, but am not yet completely sure, that it all has to do with something you can upload called False Note. I don't know what that is yet, but I think we can assume it is not good. And I think there are hundreds of ***SHADOW*** agents here, A1, all wearing pink hair and all waiting for the code in the final song."

"You must find out about that code before they do, EJ," said A1.

"I know. When the band goes back on after intermission I'm going backstage to see if I can. Oh, and A1?"

"Yes, EJ?"

"You know that download link you received with the Pink Shadows song? I don't think you should open that."

"No," said A1, "neither do I. Well done, EJ12, and be careful," said A1. "SHINE out."

Through the door, EJ heard an announcement in the foyer. "Please take your seats. The Pink Shadows' final performance is about to recommence. You won't want to miss it."

I might just have to, thought EJ. There was no time to lose.

Still outside, EJ walked around to the back of the stadium, following the signs to the backstage door. This is where the bands performing could enter and leave the stadium without having to push through crowds of fans. With her pass, EJ had no problems getting past the security guard. She simply smiled and flashed the pass and the woman smiled back as she stepped aside and opened the door for her. Too easy. EJ was in, but where should she go now?

She could hear the Pink Shadows playing so she followed the sound until she was standing on the side of the stage. She could see all the spotlights and ropes for the curtains and, most excitingly, she could see the band. EJ wished she could stay and watch the show, but she needed to find out what was going on before the band came off the stage. EJ stepped back and slipped around to the back of the stage area. She saw a door and a sign to the dressing rooms. *Perfect*, she thought. *If I can get into Shady Lady's dressing room, maybe I can find out what False Note is.* She slowly turned the doorknob, opened the door a fraction and peered through the crack. There were more doors. One had a pink and black star on it and a sign.

And sitting on a chair to the side of the door, there was another security guard, bigger, stronger and, this time, not very friendly looking at all. EJ knew her backstage pass wasn't going to work here, but she had to get into that dressing room. But how? EJ thought hard. *What would work?* Then, as she fiddled with her charm bracelet, she saw the little microphone. Of course! It was time for micro-speak. EJ took the charm and twisted it. The charm expanded to the size of a real microphone, but on its side was a dial. There were more than twenty voice types around the dial and then another dial for voice style. There were many possible combinations: baby tired, baby excited, very old woman excited or angry or whispering, young girls, whispering or sad or excited (*they could use Isi for that one*, thought EJ, giggling a little to herself), young man, whispering effect. EJ fiddled the dials until she found the one she was looking for. *Here goes nothing*, she thought, as she turned the dial to woman's voice, then the next dial to loudspeaker. She turned up the volume and spoke into the microphone.

"Attention all backstage security staff!" A voice EJ didn't recognize boomed out of the microphone. *This is so cool,* thought EJ, *it doesn't sound anything like me. I sound like my mom! I could really have fun with this.* She started speaking again. "This is not a drill. We have a security breach. Report stage left immediately. I repeat, this is not a drill. All security staff report immediately."

As EJ hoped she would, the guard got up and began to run down the corridor, away from the dressing room. Quickly EJ opened the door and dashed across to Shady Lady's dressing room door. EJ turned the door handle, hoping the door would be unlocked. She was in luck, it was. EJ took a quick look up and down the corridor to check she was still alone and then turned the handle again and entered the dressing room.

She was in. And she was face-to-face with a very small but very angry Chihuahua, a Chihuahua growling at EJ and baring some unexpectedly large and sharp-looking teeth. It was Pinky-poo, Shady Lady's over-primped pooch.

The fluffy little dog was sitting, bow on its head, on a satin cushion on the dressing table in front of a large mirror surrounded by lights. EJ sniffed—the dog had even been sprayed with perfume. EJ thought dogs smelled better as dogs.

Next to Pinky-poo's cushion was a laptop computer. Not your usual rock star equipment but, as EJ now knew, Shady Lady was not your usual rock star. EJ needed to look at that laptop. She moved toward the laptop but then jumped back quickly as Pinky-poo once again growled and bared her teeth. EJ tried moving forward again, this time super slowly, but again the dog growled. How was she going to get past precious Pinky-poo?

"Hello, puppy! Aren't you a pretty puppy?" said EJ in a high-pitched voice she hoped Pinky-poo would like. Pinky-poo didn't like it and began to growl, a squeaky but still very angry growl and then she

began to yap, loudly. Really, really loudly.

"Shhh, it's okay," said EJ, fearing the noise would be heard by a security guard.

Pinky-poo obviously didn't think it was okay and yapped even more loudly than before.

"Pinky-poo, come on, please stop," pleaded EJ. Pinky-poo began to howl. This was not good. Then EJ remembered her charms. She took the dog bone charm and twisted it and waited. In a moment she was holding a small bone-shaped tin. On the tin was a label.

Chum Chews for Prickly Pups

Just one chew and you'll
be chums!

Dog treats! I really hope they're the kind she likes, thought EJ, as she unscrewed the lid and took out a little biscuit. *Yuk! It smells revolting. I hope it smells better to a dog than it does to humans,* thought EJ, scrunching up her nose.

"Here, Pinky-poo, look what I have for you," squeaked EJ, holding the biscuit as far away from her nose and as close to Pinky-poo as she could.

Pinky-poo sniffed and then, as if EJ had waved a magic wand, began wagging her tail as she jumped off the table and trotted over to EJ. Kneeling down, EJ gave her the biscuit. Pinky-poo chewed it, wagging her tail furiously—her tail with a little pink and black bow tied to it. EJ gave her another one and the dog started licking her like a new best friend. Well, a dog best friend, anyway. EJ had Pinky-poo eating out of her hand.

EJ noticed the poor dog's claws had been left long and had little stickers on them—the poor thing had been given a pedicure, no wonder she was so irritated. EJ gently peeled the stickers off Pinky-poo's claws. The Chihuahua started licking her more. As EJ lifted her head, trying to avoid the dog's licks, she noticed that the laptop screen had come on. As Pinky-poo had jumped, she must have hit one of the laptop keys. There in the middle of the screen was a single word that EJ knew all too well, and below it, something else in small writing. She tucked Pinky-poo under her arm and crossed to the laptop. Leaning closer to it she read the small writing.

"Good girl, Pinky," said EJ, taking the pink and black bow off the dog's tail and giving the dog a pat. "I think you would make a great SHINE agent."

Chapter 10

EJ clicked on the mail message. The screen flashed and a prompt appeared.

PASSWORD REQUESTED

EJ thought that might happen. What would Shady Lady's password be? EJ looked at the little dog now sitting on the floor happily chewing on one of Shady Lady's boots and smiled as she keyed in

P-I-N-K-Y-P-O-O. She hit enter. The email opened.

"Too easy!" said EJ. "Thanks again, Pinky." The email was short but very informative.

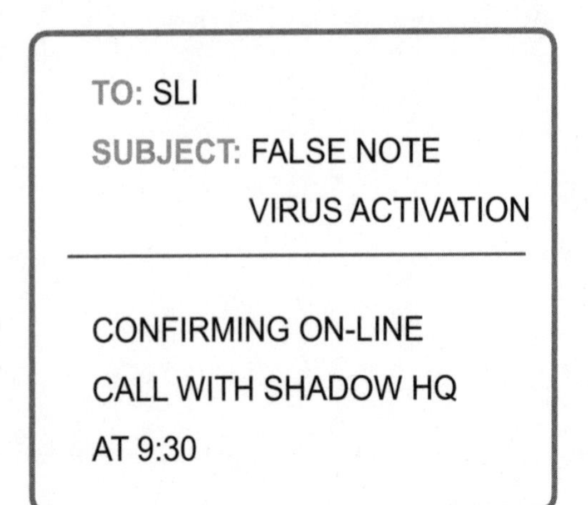

SL1—that must be Shady Lady's code name. EJ checked the time. It was 9:25, which meant Shady Lady would be here at any minute. Then EJ heard the audience roar. A moment later EJ heard footsteps coming along the corridor. The second half of the show was over and the band had left the stage. Shady Lady and the others were coming back to their dressing rooms to get ready for the encore,

the final song. And EJ was standing in Shady Lady's dressing room. This was not good. EJ closed the message and marked it as unread; she didn't want Shady Lady to know someone had read it. She also didn't want Shady Lady to find her in the dressing room. EJ looked around for somewhere to hide. There were costumes and guitars everywhere... Then EJ saw another door with another sign.

The footsteps were getting louder. EJ had no time to think of anywhere else to go. She also realized that Shady Lady would see that Pinky-poo's bow and stickers had been removed. She scooped up Pinky-poo, opened the door, darted through, then quietly shut it behind her. As that door shut, the dressing room door opened and Shady Lady burst in. EJ activated the hyper-hear listening device on her spy-pod and could hear every word Shady Lady said.

"Pinky-poo! Come here my baby. Pinky-poo! Where are you, darling?" called Shady Lady. "Hiding again, you naughty little girl! Well, Mommy will find you, but right now clever Mommy has a secret agency to shut down." She laughed to herself as she sat at her laptop and dialed in for her call with ***SHADOW HQ***.

"This is Shady Lady, rock star and ***SHADOW*** agent of the year reporting in to ***SHADOW HQ*** about False Note."

A voice came through the laptop speakers. "Voice recognition confirmed. Proceed with report, SL1."

"***SHADOW*** agents are in place in the stadium and ready to receive the final upload code for False Note," said Shady Lady. "We have instructed them using Headset Hair. My compliments to whoever came up with that idea."

"We will pass the compliment on to AX," said the voice. "Please continue with your report."

EJ jumped when she heard that. AX? It was Adriana. She hadn't wasted much time after her last plan, Operation Lights Out, had failed. And, as EJ remembered back to her mission in Black Cave Mine, did that explain why Adriana had been listening to the Pink Shadows music? Had she been working on Headset Hair then?

"Just to recap," continued Shady Lady, "little bits of the code for the computer virus False Note have been encoded into all our songs. With so many of the songs downloaded, there are now bits of code sitting on thousands of computers everywhere. The False Note virus has grown and has been spread further than we could have hoped and is now ready for activation. Once activated, the False Note virus will invade each computer's hard drive and scramble everything. The computers will be useless."

EJ was listening, stunned, not only to what Shady Lady was saying, but to her voice. She sounded nothing like the rock star on television, instead she

was very precise and businesslike. EJ felt a little sad. The Pink Shadows was one of her favorite bands. Was the band nothing more than a cover for an evil spy agency or was it just Shady Lady? Her mom had never liked Shady Lady, she always said you couldn't trust someone in heels that high.

Shady Lady continued her report. "We have managed to email hundreds of agents inside SHINE and plant bits of the virus code. The silly SHINE agents have downloaded them themselves, thinking they are just song downloads. By sending the virus out in small parts, we have been able to escape detection by virus protection software. It is, simply, brilliant."

A1's email, thought EJ. *Even A1 is building the virus!* Then she thought of her family's computer at home. *We are building the virus. Millions of people will be.*

"Excellent work," the voice replied to Shady Lady. "We are impressed."

"I look forward to seeing just how impressed when I check my bank account," said Shady.

"The final song tonight has been rewritten with the upload code. Once our agents upload it, the virus will be activated and nothing will be able to stop it. I am sending through the code now. It will rock SHINE completely. False Note will shut SHINE down and no one will ever know how it happened."

Except for me, thought EJ. *I have to work out how to stop Shady Lady singing that final song.*

Shady Lady was still talking, but EJ had heard enough. She needed a plan and quickly. Then Pinky-poo barked.

"Shhh, Pinky, not now, she will hear you. Oh, no she won't," said EJ remembering the soundproof room. "But that has given me an idea," she said, as she looked at her spy-pod. "Okay, Pinky, now bark!" EJ held up a Chum Chew and Pinky barked with excitement. EJ recorded it on her spy-pod then gave Pinky the treat. She then linked her spy-pod to

her micro-speak and recorded the barking. She set the micro-speak for repeat play, pushed the pause button then placed the micro-speak in the far corner of the room.

"Just one more thing," said EJ, as she turned the light off. Then, just to make sure it stayed dark, EJ clicked her sneakers again, waited for the heels to fully extend before stretching up, holding Pinky with one hand and removing the bulb from the light with the other. The practice room was now in complete darkness but, as an experienced night mission agent, EJ could handle that.

Still holding Pinky under one arm, she quietly opened the door between the practice room and the dressing room, just a little, then activated the play button on the micro-speak with her spy-pod remote. EJ hid behind the door. The noise of Pinky barking filled the room.

"Oh, Pinky-poo, is that you, darling?" cried Shady Lady getting up and moving toward the practice room. "What are you doing in there, you naughty dog? You know you are not supposed to leave your cushion!"

Come on, Shady Lady, keep walking, thought EJ, *keep walking.*

Shady Lady was moving closer toward the practice room. EJ held her breath—and gave Pinky another treat to keep her occupied.

"I can't see you, Pinky, the light isn't working. Come on, Pinky-poo, come to Mommy."

The micro-speak kept playing the barking noise and Shady Lady kept walking toward it. EJ could sense Shady Lady was nearly at the back of the room. Like lightning and with Pinky under her arm, EJ stepped out from behind the practice room door and into the dressing room, shutting and then locking the door behind her. Shady Lady had been locked in the practice room—the soundproof practice room. EJ put her spy-pod against the wall and did a quick check with her hyper-hear.

"Hey, what's happening? Let me out! Don't you know who I am? I have an encore to sing!" shouted Shady Lady.

"I certainly do know who you are and you won't be singing any encore," said EJ, although she knew

that Shady Lady couldn't hear her. "The only singing you'll be doing will be in a SHINE security center."

Pinky-poo jumped onto her cushion and EJ went over to Shady Lady's laptop. Sitting on the desktop was the remix of "Rock 'n' Shine" with the new lyrics. Somewhere in those lyrics was the upload code.

EJ studied the words. It was only the first part that was different, so that must be the bit that contained the upload code. The words to the last song of the last concert that contained the last code. Last, the last word... Could that be it? EJ took the mouse and highlighted the last word of every line in the song.

Once EJ had highlighted the last word of every line of the song she then copied the words down onto the back of her concert ticket.

Up load one for to one rock shine Now don't wait rock shine

EJ was disappointed; she had been so sure that she had cracked the code. She read the words again, and then she smiled as she wrote the words out again, only in a slightly different way this time.

Up load 1 4 2 1 rock shine

That was it, EJ knew it would be, the final upload code that would rock the SHINE network: 1-4-2-1. Except now it wouldn't rock anything.

Feeling rather happy with herself, EJ called A1.

"Hello, EJ12. How are you doing? What do we know about False Note?" asked A1.

"Quite a bit. I have discovered what False Note is. It's a computer virus that has been sent out in Pink Shadows songs."

"But surely our virus software would have picked it up," said A1.

"No, that is where *SHADOW* has been really clever. It only becomes a virus once the final code has been uploaded and that was going to be given to *SHADOW* agents in the last song at the concert tonight. The song had been rewritten to include the upload code. Once the *SHADOW* agents received it through their crazy hair and headsets, they would upload it to the Internet, activating False Note, causing computer chaos everywhere. But not anymore," said EJ, feeling rather pleased with herself.

"Well done, EJ12! You have done a fabulous job," said A1. "But there is just one more thing we need to do to bring the curtain down on *SHADOW*."

"What's that, A1?" asked EJ, worried that she had forgotten something.

"Well, I was just thinking, shouldn't that final song be playing now?" asked A1.

"Well it should be, but it won't because I have Shady Lady locked in her own practice room. She will not be singing any more songs. She won't be going anywhere."

"Good work, EJ," said A1, "but..."

"Yes, A1?" asked EJ. *Have I forgotten something else?* she wondered to herself.

"Don't worry, EJ, you haven't forgotten anything, but we still have a problem. If Shady Lady doesn't go back on stage for her encore, the **SHADOW** agents will become suspicious. We don't want that." A1 was silent for a moment "No, EJ, I have an idea. The show must go on. The show will go on. The final song must be sung but not with the message the **SHADOW** agents are expecting."

"Great idea!" cried EJ, who seemed to know what A1 was thinking. "We can send them a new message, something that will make them come right to us. We will be able to arrest all those **SHADOW** agents."

"Exactly," said A1. "Great minds think alike, EJ12."

"That's brilliant, A1, but who will sing the new

message?" asked EJ12. She couldn't think who SHINE would be able to send.

"Oh, I would have thought that was obvious, EJ12. You, of course."

That was not obvious and it was no longer a great idea. A1 had to be kidding.

But EJ knew she wasn't. A1 didn't kid on missions.

Chapter 11

A1's plan made perfect sense. EJ would change the words of the song to set a trap for the *SHADOW* agents. Rather than give them the upload code, a new message would direct them all backstage, where SHINE would be waiting for them.

As Shady Lady changed her clothes and make-up several times during a concert, no one would notice if she wasn't wearing the same outfit when she returned for the encore. EJ could simply change into one of her costumes and create a mask with makeup so the audience wouldn't be able to tell that it wasn't Shady Lady on stage. EJ could then use her guitar charm to be able to "play" Shady Lady's guitar. It all made perfect sense—right up until the part where it was EJ singing the song.

EJ took a deep breath. "A1, I don't think I can do the last bit. Why don't I just change the code and someone else can come and sing the song? I don't know, perhaps someone who has performed a concert in a stadium before?" She wanted to add, "Perhaps someone who didn't ruin a kindergarten concert," but didn't.

"There's no time for that, EJ. Shady Lady should be on stage right now and you are the only agent we have there. Just stay calm, EJ, and take one step at a time. Change the song code, then change into your costume and then pop on stage and sing the song. Good luck, EJ12. SHINE out."

"Pop on stage and sing the song," mumbled EJ a bit crossly. "That's easy for you to say. But okay, one step at a time, let's look at the song. I need to change the first five lines to make a message from the last words of each line. Hmm."

EJ looked at the lyrics, thought for a bit, then scribbled some new words down.

Don't wait.
Don't hold back.
Light up the stage.
We're gonna rock to the end.
We're gonna rock this show!

They weren't the most fantastic song words, but at least the code worked. EJ double checked it, just to make sure.

Don't wait.
Don't hold back.
Light up the stage.
We're gonna rock to the end.
We're gonna rock this show!

Wait backstage end show

That should do it, thought EJ.

And then the rest of the chorus was the same, just like in Shady Lady's version.

We're gonna rock.
It's our time to shine.

No, actually, thought EJ, *it's* ***SHADOW*** *who is going to be rocked and* ***SHINE's*** *time to shine!*

Next EJ needed to change. It was lucky Shady Lady was so small because EJ could wear her costumes. She picked out some leather pants, a purple tank top and some necklaces. On her right arm, where Shady Lady had her tattoo, EJ put on a black armband. Then, using the stage makeup on the table, EJ began to draw. On her face. She drew pink, purple and orange swirls around her eyes until it was as if she was wearing a mask, a mask that would stop anyone guessing that she wasn't Shady Lady, at least for a little while.

EJ picked up one of Shady Lady's guitars and, using her spy-pod and guitar charm, uploaded "Rock 'n' Shine" for lead guitar. She would now "play" like a rock goddess, just like Shady Lady.

But EJ didn't feel like a rock goddess and didn't think she could perform like one either. Maybe in her bedroom she could but not in a packed stadium.

EJ12 was going to need some help. A lot of help.

"Shady! Shady! Shady!"

The crowd's chants were getting louder and were sounding slightly impatient.

EJ was still in the dressing room. She would very much like to have stayed there but knew she had to go on stage. She had to deliver the message, she just didn't know how she was going to be able to. What if she just froze, like she did in the kindergarten concert? Or forgot the words—that would be a disaster. Everyone would know she wasn't Shady

Lady and the **SHADOW** agents would escape. *But hold on a moment,* she thought to herself, *I know the words, and I know them backward. Elle and I sing this song all the time.*

Elle, that was exactly who EJ needed. She took out her phone and called her BESTie.

"Hi there." Elle's voice was bright and cheery despite it being quite late. "How can I help?"

EJ didn't really know where to start. "Elle, why don't you mind singing in front of people?"

"I don't really think about the other people, I just think about the song and the music. Why? What made you think about that? I thought you were OM?" said Elle.

OM was how EJ and her BESTies described EJ being on a mission. They'd made it up themselves and thought it sounded very spy-like, very secret.

"I am," replied EJ, "that's why I need to know."

"Okay, well," said Elle, "actually I don't think about the people at all, I think about the song. I get lost in the song. Does that help?"

"Sort of," replied EJ.

"There's something else that might help," said Elle. "My mom used to say that you should try to imagine the audience in their underwear, then you can't possibly be nervous about them because they look so silly." She giggled.

EJ giggled too. She felt better just talking to her friend. "I'm not sure that helps, Elle, but it is funny."

"Hey, you're not still worried about the talent concert are you?"

"Well no, actually, yes," replied EJ, "but this is another concert, and a little bigger than the school one."

"How much bigger?"

"A lot," said EJ, "like a whole stadium bigger."

"You are kidding me!" cried Elle. Then she paused before talking again. "Hang on, you're at the Pink Shadows concert aren't you? I know, you can't answer that, but you have to be. I can't believe it, you are so lucky!" shrieked Elle. "That is so cool, you are like a real rock star!"

"Yeah, a rock star who is too shy to sing," said EJ glumly. "Elle, I just don't think I can even walk out

on stage, let alone sing and I have to sing 'Rock 'n' Shine.' Now. And I can't."

"You can and hey, I have an idea," said Elle. "Why don't we sing it together, just like in your room?"

"How?"

"You still have that fancy phone, right?" said her friend.

"Yes."

"Okay, keep me on the phone and plug in your earphones and I'll sing with you—we'll sing a secret duet. Hey, then I will be a rock star too! What do you think?"

EJ thought it was a fantastic idea. With her friend singing with her, she thought she just might be able to do it. As she took out her phone, she noticed the little heart charm on her bracelet and twisted it. As she did, an inscription appeared,

Never be too shy to shine.

EJ smiled. With the help of her friend she just might be able to shine after all. She plugged in her earphones.

"Are you still there, Elle?" she checked.

"Are you kidding, where would I go? I wouldn't miss this for anything. This is going to be so cool, just wait until we tell..."

"Elle!" said EJ. "You know you mustn't tell anyone about this, ever."

"I know, sorry, just forgot. My lips are sealed. Well, after we've finished singing they will be!"

"Okay, well here goes," said EJ quietly. She got up, tickled Pinky-poo under her chin and left the dressing room. "I'm walking up the corridor and onto the side of the stage. The lights are so bright, Elle." EJ could feel her mouth go dry as she spoke.

"Awesome," cried Elle. "What are we waiting for? Let's go!"

EJ walked on stage, and the crowd went crazy. The other members of the band looked at EJ and then looked at each other. Could they tell? If they could, it was too late—a spotlight shone onto EJ as she stepped up to the microphone.

"Here we go, Elle," she whispered to her friend. "Stay with me, won't you?"

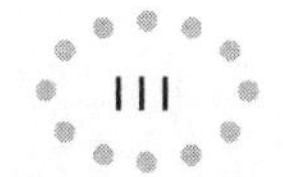

"I'm here, all the time. Let's rock!"

EJ took a deep breath, pressed play on the guitar charm and spoke into the microphone. "Here's one last song for all you **SHADOWs** out there. It's a special remix of 'Rock 'n' Shine'!"

The crowd roared. EJ waited for the drums to start, then the bass, then the keyboard. Then EJ's guitar let rip and she and Elle began to sing. Even though they were right in front of her, EJ didn't really see the audience, she didn't notice the spotlights or the lasers. She didn't even really notice the other band members, who were giving her slightly odd looks. She just sang, she sang her heart out with her BESTie, just like in her bedroom, although with better speakers! And EJ loved it, she loved every minute of it. The crowd did too, but all too soon it was over. The moment the song finished, the stadium went black and all EJ could see was a steady stream of fluorescent pink hair moving toward the backstage area. The plan was working like a song.

EJ had done it.

"Thanks heaps, Elle," whispered EJ. "I've got it

from here. See you at school."

As the stage lights came back on and the audience began to leave, EJ quickly slipped back to Shady Lady's dressing room. She had one more thing to do.

Chapter 13

Back in the dressing room, Pinky-poo was excited to see EJ and another Chum Chew made her even more so. EJ took out her phone and pressed 4-6-6-3 into the keypad and a woman's voice answered immediately.

"SHINE Home Delivery Service—straight to your door anytime, anywhere."

"Agent EJ12 requesting home delivery, express please," replied EJ.

"Roger that," said the woman, "and for how many this time, EJ12?"

EJ thought, she wasn't completely sure. "Maybe about 500," she said.

"Oh, we've already started rounding the *SHADOW* agents up. They were easy to see with that pink hair! We also picked up Shady Lady earlier. Good job, EJ12. This mission should see you win big points in the Shining Stars competition. So, is it just you for the limo?"

"Well," started EJ.

"EJ12?"

"Just one extra," she said looking at Pinky. "Shady seems to have left her dog behind."

"Okay, EJ, make your way to the back of the stadium. Agent REV1 is waiting for you there. SHINE out."

EJ changed back into her clothes and removed her makeup. With Pinky under her arm, she left the dressing room and headed for the backstage door. Sure enough, the long white limo was waiting outside, with Agent REV1 standing by the open door.

"Well done, EJ," she smiled. "I saw you from the back of the stadium. You were awesome. Do you think you might take on the role of lead singer of the Pink Shadows permanently? I hear there's a vacancy and having seen you perform, you would be great."

"Thanks, but I don't think so," laughed EJ, as she got into the car. "I think I'll stick to school concerts."

"Well settle back and enjoy the drive home," said Agent REV1.

EJ did just that. She made herself another raspberry lemonade and relaxed. Then her phone rang. It was A1.

"Well done, EJ12. Another outstanding mission."

"Thanks, A1. What about the False Note virus? Were we able to stop it?" asked EJ.

"Stop it and destroy it," reassured A1. "It's all gone. We have been able to clean it from the Internet and Shady Lady is now singing solo under **SHINE** guard. You will be pleased to know that the other band members didn't know anything about Shady Lady's plot so you haven't lost one of your favorite bands after all. They will find a new lead singer and be back on the charts in no time, I am sure."

EJ smiled. "That's great. I won't miss Shady Lady, but I was going to miss the Pink Shadows' songs. They're fantastic."

"Yes, they are quite groovy," agreed A1. EJ smiled at A1's choice of adjective as A1 continued, "Oh, and one more thing, EJ."

"Yes A1?"

"A message from your mom: no more pets."

"Oh no," said EJ, looking at Pinky.

"Don't worry, Agent REV1 has been looking for a little dog. I think she may have just found one. That's all, EJ12. SHINE out."

The driver's window slid back. "I'll take good care of her, EJ," said Agent REV1. "No more perfume and pedicures and definitely no more being squashed into handbags. She will get plenty of exercise. But you should get some rest now. I hear you have a big week coming up."

The talent competition. EJ had nearly forgotten about that. But now, as she stretched out to take a nap, she realized that she wasn't nervous, just excited. She couldn't wait to perform with her friends.

And she had a great idea about how Squishy Music could do their song.

The next Friday at school was the big day, the We've Got Talent competition. The school hall had been set up like a concert stadium and was packed with students and parents. The atmosphere was electric!

Squishy Music was backstage waiting to go on. The girls' act was after the boy burping the alphabet and before the duo pretending to be leaves. Emma had butterflies in her stomach, but they were the excited butterflies not the really nervous ones.

"Hey, where's Nema and her band?" asked Emma. "I can't see them listed on the program."

"No, they split up," said Hannah. "Apparently Nema got too bossy, even for the Nemettes, so they left the band. When Nema tried to register as a solo act, the teachers said it was too late."

"Oh, that's a pity," said Emma. Even though she didn't think Nema had been very nice, she did feel a little sorry for her.

"Maybe she will be less bossy to her friends now," said Hannah. "How good would it be if Nema was nice again?"

Emma agreed, but she wouldn't count on it happening. Nema just seemed to be bossy all the time these days. Emma missed the old Nema.

"Anyway, who's going to be the lead singer?" asked Isi. "We still haven't decided."

"You don't have to do it if you don't want to, Em," said Hannah.

"No, it's fine, Han, it is really. And, actually, I had an idea," said Emma. "Why don't Elle and I do it together as a duet?"

"That could be amazing," agreed Isi, "but have you practiced?"

"I think we will be okay," said Emma, smiling at her friend, who was beaming right back at her.

There was a teacher talking on stage, introducing the next act.

"Hey, that's us," said Elle. "Come on!"

Hannah came up and put her arm around Emma. "Good idea about the duet, Em, but are you sure you are okay?" she asked.

"Absolutely," said Emma, "with a little help from Elle and all of you."

And, she thought to herself, *EJ12.*

Book 1!

The heat is on as someone seems to be melting the polar ice cap.

Special Agent EJ12 needs to crack the codes and keep her cool to put the evildoer's plan back on ice.
That's the easy part.

As EJ12, Emma Jacks can do anything.

So why can't she handle the school Ice Queen of Mean, Nema?

Perhaps she can after all...

Book 2!

Evil agency SHADOW is up to something in the middle of the rain forest. Something that could see them get the jump on SHINE.

Special Agent EJ12 needs to leap into action. She must crack SHADOW's codes and trust her instincts to foil their plans and save the rain forest.

That's the easy part.
As EJ12, Emma Jacks can do anything.

So why is the state gymnastics meet so hard?

Perhaps it isn't after all...

Book 3!

SHINE's solar energy station is under threat from the evil agency SHADOW. Special Agent EJ12 needs to lighten up. She must crack their codes and overcome her fears to stop them before they turn the lights out on the SHINE network.

That's the easy part.
As EJ12, Emma Jacks can do anything.

So why is she worried about going to her best friend's slumber party?

Perhaps she isn't after all...